PAPER PLANES

Jim Helmore and Richard Jones

SIMON & SCHUSTER
London   New York   Sydney   Toronto   New Delhi

Mia and Ben were the very best of friends.

They lived side by side on the edge of a great, wide lake.

Together they sailed . . .

. . . and swung and sang,

but what they loved
to do most of all was
make paper planes.

In the winter, when geese flocked to the lake,
Mia and Ben would race their planes with the birds above.

And in the summer, when the geese had gone, they would climb
into the hills and watch their planes circle slowly home.

Perhaps, one day, they would make a plane
that could fly all the way over the lake . . .

Then the friends heard some terrible news:
Ben had to leave.
His family was moving to a new home,
a long way away.

Mia and Ben felt crushed.

How could they stay best friends if they were so far apart?

They promised never
to forget one another,

swapping planes
before saying goodbye.

As the days passed,
Mia missed Ben very much.

Way over the sea, in a busy city,
Ben was lonely too.

Winter arrived.

When the geese came back,
Mia would have to race them on her own.

Hot, angry tears
fell from her eyes.

They would never make a plane that could fly
across the lake now.

Mia took the plane that Ben had given her
and smashed it on the ground.

That night, as moonlight crept across her bedroom floor,
Mia heard something.

Was it the wind?

No! It was the sound of distant geese
calling and the beat of powerful wings.

Down in the garden, she spied the broken plane,
but it looked different somehow . . .

Mia hurried outside for a closer look.
Ben's plane was as good as new!

The swish and chatter of geese grew louder
and a wild wind began to blow.

As the wind whipped around its wings,
the plane started to get bigger . . .

Soon it was large enough
for Mia to climb aboard.

Then one huge gust
whisked her up into the air.

The geese were right overhead now, their feathers shining silver in the light of the moon.

Climbing at terrific speed, Mia joined the flock.

Crossing land and sea,
they rushed through the night.

Up ahead, Mia saw something else in the sky.
Could it be . . . ?

Yes! It was the plane she had given Ben,
and there was Ben, waving and smiling!

The two pilots flew fearlessly together . . .

swooping and
skimming

and soaring.

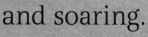

Mia wished they could stay forever,

but as the sun began to rise, she knew it was time to go.

And in the beat of a wing . . .

. . . Mia found herself back in her bedroom,

with Ben's plane in
the palm of her hand.

At breakfast time, a parcel arrived for her.
Inside was a brand new plane . . . but it had no wings.

There was also a note, which read:

Dear Mia, I really need
your help to finish this.
No one else can make wings
like you!
Love Ben

Mia remembered her flight with the geese,
how their long necks stretched and their wide wings beat.
And over the weeks she worked and worked and worked.

In the springtime, Mia took the new plane down to the water's
edge and threw it up into the air.

Soaring higher than any plane they had ever made before,
it swooped above the last of the geese . . .

. . . and flew all the way across the lake!

Mia and Ben could still make planes together.

The best planes in the world!

They would always be friends.
They would never be too far apart.

For Phoebe,
Émile and Evan – JH

For Toby – RJ

SIMON & SCHUSTER
First published in Great Britain in 2019 by Simon & Schuster UK Ltd,
1st Floor, 222 Gray's Inn Road, London WC1X 8HB • A CBS Company
Text copyright © 2019 Jim Helmore • Illustrations copyright © 2019
Richard Jones • The right of Jim Helmore and Richard Jones to be identified
as the author and illustrator of this work has been asserted by them in
accordance with the Copyright, Designs and Patents Act, 1988 • All rights
reserved, including the right of reproduction in whole or in part in any
form • A CIP catalogue record for this book is available from the British
Library upon request • Printed in China • ISBN: 978-1-4711-7388-2 (HB)
ISBN: 978-1-4711-7387-5 (PB) • ISBN: 978-1-4711-7389-9 (eBook)
10 9 8 7 6 5 4 3 2 1